The Whistling Monster

Stories from Around the World

JAMILA GAVIN

The
**Whistling
Monster**

Stories from
Around the World

illustrated by
Suzanne Barrett

WALKER
BOOKS

For Jessica, with love
J.G.

For Finn, Mum and Dad
S.B.

First published in Great Britain 1997 as *Our Favourite Stories* by Dorling Kindersley Ltd

This edition published 2009 by Walker Books Ltd
87 Vauxhall Walk, London SE11 5HJ

10

Text © 1997 Jamila Gavin
Illus

LONDON BOROUGH OF WANDSWORTH	
9030 00007 0625 7	
Askews & Holts	27-Feb-2020
JF	£5.99
	WW19017776

ISBN 978-1-4063-1994-1

www.walker.co.uk

MIX
Paper from
responsible sources
FSC
www.fsc.org FSC® C020471

Contents

Introduction

All over the world, children love stories. They inherit a huge storehouse from the religion, history and folk traditions of their cultures. The stories in this book come from all corners of the globe: a folktale from Finland, a creation myth from the Canadian Inuit, a religious story from India. Their roots lie deep in spiritual or cultural ground and their themes will be recognized everywhere: the battle between good and evil, the perils of disobedience and disrespect for nature, the importance of bravery and wisdom. Full of mystery, wit and wisdom, these tales have survived hundreds of years of retelling to become favourites all around the world.

The Whistling Monster
A STORY FROM BRAZIL

Deep in the forest, where wonderful
creatures creep, crawl, swoop and shimmer,
where the River Amazon winds like a great
serpent, lived a boy called Kanassa.

Kanassa was always boasting: how he
climbed the highest trees looking for honey,

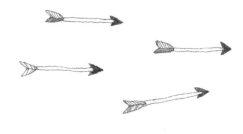

how no one in his village
was more skilful than he at catching
fish. He often aimed his arrows at
the birds of the forest – the parrots and
toucans and cockatoos – which annoyed
them very much.

One day, a huge, silver fish was sighted
upriver.

"I'll catch that fish!" boasted Kanassa.

"Oh, Kanassa!" wailed his mother.

"Oh, Kanassa!" wailed his sister.

"Oh, Kanassa!" wailed his old
grandmother. "Don't go too far up the river,
or the Whistling Monster might get you."

Kanassa laughed. "Don't worry, I'm not
afraid of monsters!"

He painted his face and body to show he was brave. He filled a *cabaça* with fresh water and stored bananas and gourds in his canoe. Then, taking his bow and his sharpest arrows, Kanassa paddled away upriver.

He paddled for three days, but there was no sign of the fish. Then on the fourth day he spotted it – shining like a moon and big enough to feed a village. Kanassa stood, feet apart, the canoe so perfectly balanced, there was not one ripple in the water. He fitted an arrow to his bow and aimed. Just as he was about to let fly, from out of the forest came a long, low, eerie whistle. The sound froze his blood.

He fell back, terrified. Rising through the trees, he saw a coil of smoke. Kanassa paddled ashore.

"Someone in this village might know who made that strange noise."

He walked deep into the forest, till he came to a group of mud huts. An old man was sitting near by.

"Please, sir, what creature is it making that whistling sound?" asked Kanassa.

The old man looked scared. "Go home, boy! Go home. No one who crosses the path of the Whistling Monster lives to tell the tale."

Huh! thought Kanassa. I'm not afraid of monsters. And he decided to carry on fishing.

On the way back to the river, the forest got darker and darker. His feet padded through the undergrowth. Other footsteps followed him. Kanassa stopped and listened. The footsteps stopped. Then he heard the whistling, not far away. Kanassa began to run. The footsteps behind him ran too. The whistling got louder; he could almost feel its breath in his ear. Kanassa fell in terror behind a banana plant and pulled its leaves around him. Then he saw it. It was horrible. It was worse than anything the elders of the village had ever warned him of. It was wildly hairy; tall as a giant, with claws instead of hands and a terrible tail which thrashed about. But worst of all was the hole in its head, and from out of the hole came the whistling sound.

13

Kanassa shivered. Kanassa shook. The leaves rattled with his fear. The monster saw him.

"Run, Kanassa, run!" screamed a voice in his head. Kanassa ran. The monster followed, crashing and thundering behind him. The terrible whistling got closer and closer and closer.

"Help me! Help me!" yelled Kanassa to anyone who would listen. The birds of the forest heard him.

"Why should we help you? You only aim arrows at us!"

"I promise I never will again!" pleaded Kanassa.

So the birds decided to help.

They flew in like a mighty wind, fluttering, pecking and scratching.

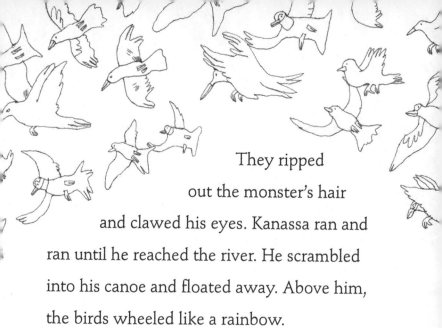

They ripped
out the monster's hair
and clawed his eyes. Kanassa ran and
ran until he reached the river. He scrambled
into his canoe and floated away. Above him,
the birds wheeled like a rainbow.

"Thank you!" cried Kanassa.

"No fish?" scoffed the people when
he returned.

"No fish,"
mumbled Kanassa.
"But I saw the
Whistling Monster
and lived to tell
the tale."

The Corn Maidens

A STORY FROM MEXICO

Life, till then, had been hard. Sometimes the sun burned so fiercely, the ground cracked; the rain didn't fall for months on end and the streams dried up. Worst of all, the corn didn't grow, and the people nearly starved.

Then the Corn Maidens came: six sisters, dancing hand in hand in the fields. Their bare feet thudded in the deep furrows of the

earth and they turned their glistening faces
to the sky and sang, "Come, sun! Come,
rain! Make the corn grow."

The sun shone for them and the rain
rained. The corn grew tall and the villagers
reaped an abundance of grain.

"Stay with us for ever," begged the
villagers. "We will build you a house and
feed you, and we will always respect you."

So every year the Corn Maidens danced
in the fields and every year the corn grew
tall. But as the people grew prosperous,
they became neglectful. One year, the Corn

Maidens danced, but the people forgot about leaving them any food and stopped being respectful. The Corn Maidens were saddened, then angry. The eldest sister, Yellow Corn, said, "We must leave this place. Let the people see what happens when we are not here."

Before the mists of morning had lifted, the six Corn Maidens took the road south. They went to Pautiwa, the spirit man. "Please hide us until the people have learnt they cannot prosper without us."

Pautiwa led the six Corn Maidens to the shores of a shining water and transformed himself into a duck. Drawing the sisters under one wing, he sank with them to the bottom of the lake.

At first, the villagers didn't notice that the Corn Maidens had gone. They carried on, confident that the corn would flourish as usual. But when harvest came, the crop was poor; the next year it was worse, and the year after it failed altogether.

The people went to their priest. "Help us!" they cried. "Even though the sun shone and the rains came, our corn withered. What can we do?"

"Where are the Corn Maidens?" asked the priest.

The villagers looked around. "We didn't need them any more. All they did was dance. We were the ones who worked day and night in the fields. They must have gone."

"Find them," ordered the priest.

The villagers searched in every direction, but in vain. Then someone said, "We must go to Paiyatuma, the magic musician. Only he can help us."

Paiyatuma lived high among the rocks near the head of a waterfall, beneath the arch of an everlasting rainbow. As the people toiled up the hill, they heard him playing his flute. His music was magic. Nothing could  resist its power. Paiyatuma sat crowned with flowers and encircled by butterflies.

"O Paiyatuma, O most gracious musician, blessed by the gods, we are starving because the Corn Maidens have run away. Please help us find them."

Paiyatuma prepared four prayer sticks: yellow, red, blue and white. To each he fixed an eagle's feather and set them facing to the north, south, east and west. Although the wind blew, the feathers on the yellow, blue and white sticks stayed still, but the feather on the red stick swayed to and fro.

"Ah!" smiled Paiyatuma. "Your maidens

went south. Their breath moves the feather. I'll take you to them."

Putting the flute to his lips, Paiyatuma led the villagers south, playing all the way. His notes dropped like pebbles through the shining waters of the lake, down to where the Corn Maidens lay sleeping.

The sisters awoke and wanted to dance. Pautiwa floated up with them to the surface of the lake. The people fell on their knees before the Corn Maidens and begged forgiveness. "Please come back with us," they cried. "Now we know how much we need you."

Pautiwa shook his feathers and changed back into human form, clothed in a flowing white cloak. "Yes," he told the maidens, "it is time for you to return."

Paiyatuma led the way,
playing his flute. The Corn Maidens danced
behind him, followed by the villagers.
Pautiwa went last. They reached the village.
There was such joy, the celebrations lasted
all night. But, just before dawn, the Corn
Maidens placed a tray of seeds on the
ground. Paiyatuma laid his flute next to it,
then they slid away into the darkness.

"Do not fear!" Pautiwa comforted the
villagers. "Here are corn seeds and
Paiyatuma's flute. Choose
six dancing maidens and

I will stay until you have learnt the music and the dances. If you perform them faithfully every year, the corn will always grow." As the villagers learnt the songs and ceremonies, bit by bit, Pautiwa faded away like morning mist.

The villagers always remembered the Corn Maidens, and their corn always grew tall.

The Coming of Raven
A STORY FROM CANADA

Before the creation of the world, there was darkness black as Raven's wings. The darkness was Raven. Raven was Tulugaukuk, the Father of Life.

Raven spread his wings and flew down from Skyland. With mighty thrusts of his wings, he created a land called Earth. As he swooped and soared, he created the mountains, the trees and the rushing waters. Yet darkness was everywhere; black as everlasting night; black as Raven's wings. Raven longed to see his creation.

Something glinted in the ground. It was burning hot. When sparks from it flew into the air, Raven glimpsed oceans, glaciers and great forests.

"With this rock, I will be able to see what I have made," cawed Raven joyfully.

He plunged towards the fiery rock, clasped it in his claws and threw it up in the sky. The rock was the sun.

The sun gave out a mighty light. Raven saw his marvellous creation: jungles, seas, deserts and grasslands.

Pop! Raven turned in time to see a giant plant pod burst open. Out tumbled the first living creature. It was naked and frightened; it was a man, the first Inuit. The man crawled about and then stood on two legs, and with two hands reached about for food to eat. He bawled loudly, "I am cold, I am hungry. I am lonely!"

"Oh dear," sighed Raven, and he created caribou, seal, whale, walrus, bear and ox. Now the man could hunt for food and clothes.

"But I have no weapons to hunt with," cried the man.

"That is true," agreed Raven. "If I show you how to make a bow and arrows and a spear, will you promise not to kill more animals than you need to live?"

"I promise!" said the man.

So Raven showed the Inuit how to make a bow and arrows and a spear.

"And who will look after the fire while I'm away hunting? And who will keep me company through the long, cold nights?" wailed the man.

Raven flapped his wings and created a woman.

In time, there were more men and women, and they produced children. They chopped down forests to make houses; they made thread out of the sinews of animals and needles from their bones. They killed more and more animals. The Earth, sea and sky were plundered as the people became greedy, always wanting more. Earth cried out in pain and Raven heard its cry.

"Do you not remember your promise, oh Inuit people," cawed Raven angrily, "only to take what you need?"

But by this time the Inuit people no longer listened to Raven. They had forgotten their promise, and did not care about anything except their own desires. So Raven took a bag made from caribou skin. He soared towards the sun, grabbed it, stuffed it into the bag and flew back to Skyland. The world was plunged into darkness.

"Oh, oh, oh!" howled the Inuit. "We can't see, we can't keep warm, please give us back the sun."

So every now and then, Raven took pity on the people and uncovered the  sun for a few days to allow them to hunt.

Now Raven thought he should have a companion. So he took Snow Goose to be his wife, and they had a son called Raven Boy. Sometimes, Raven showed his son the caribou skin bag and the sun inside it. Raven Boy became fascinated by the fiery rock.

One day, while his father was sleeping, Raven Boy crept up to the bag, determined to open it and see the sun. But Raven woke up.

Fearful of his father's anger, Raven Boy fled with the bag to the other side of the universe and hid.

Below on Earth, without any sunshine at all, everything began to die. "Please save us, O Raven, creator of the universe. Give us back the sun!" implored the Inuit.

Raven took pity and went to look for his son. He cawed, "Raven Boy! Don't hide. Bring back the sun, or the world I created will die!"

Raven Boy heard his father's plea. He ripped open the bag and flung the sun spinning across the sky.

But so that the Inuits would remember the terror of darkness, Raven created night and day, winter and summer. And the Inuit never forgot their promise again. For ever after they respected all animals, and honoured Raven.

Puss in Boots

A STORY FROM FRANCE

A miller had three sons. He was so poor
that when he died, all he had to leave to his
sons was the mill to his eldest, a donkey to
his second, and nothing to his
third – except a cat.

"You're no use to me," said
the youngest son to the cat.
"I'm off to seek my fortune."

To the lad's amazement, the cat spoke. "Don't be in such a hurry! Give me some boots and a drawstring bag, and I'll make your fortune."

Puss got his bag and his boots and scampered off into the fields. He stuffed the bag with lettuce leaves. Silly rabbit came by and poked his nose inside to nibble. In a flash, Puss pulled the drawstring tight. He took the rabbit straight to the King and said, "Your Majesty, my master, the Marquis of Carabas, begs you to accept this humble gift."

The King was pleased. So Puss came again the next day, this time with two partridges. The King was delighted at the loyal generosity of the Marquis of Carabas.

Puss's sharp ears overheard that the King and his daughter would be out driving by the river the next day. So Puss told the miller's son to go bathing in the river. Why not? thought the lad. Puss then hid his clothes and waited for the King to come by.

Clip, clop, clippety-clop! The carriage was coming.

Puss called out, "Stop! Help! My master is drowning!" When the King saw it was Puss, he ordered his servants into the river to save the Marquis.

"Oh, sire!" cried Puss. "Some villains stole my master's clothes while he bathed."

"Do not worry, I will see to it." The King ordered a cloak to be thrown around the miller's son. Then he made room for him inside his coach. The Princess was enchanted – and straight away fell in love with the lad.

Back at the palace, the King provided the miller's son with a royal set of clothes. Now he did indeed look like the Marquis of Carabas in his velvet suit of lace and gold trimmings, his silken shirt and leather boots up to his thighs. How spectacular was the fine-feathered hat!

"I insist on driving you home," said the King. "Where do you live?"

The miller's son groaned to himself. "That's it. The game's up. I'll lose my head for sure when he sees I don't live in a castle."

But Puss replied, "My master lives in Carabas Castle. I shall go on ahead and prepare for Your Majesty's arrival."

On the way, Puss crossed meadows, fields and woods.

"If the King asks who owns all this land," he told the peasants, "just reply 'the Marquis of Carabas', or I'll have your guts for garters." Then on he went to the huge castle on top of the hill. In time, the King came by with his daughter and the miller's son.

"Who owns all this?" the King called to the peasants.

"It all belongs to the Marquis of Carabas," they dutifully replied.

"Everything I see belongs to you!" exclaimed the King admiringly, and the miller's son gave a shy shrug.

Meanwhile, Puss had reached the castle. It really belonged to a frightful man-eating ogre who had magic powers. Puss went up bravely and hammered on the door.

"Who's there?" roared the ogre.

"Me. Puss. I've heard about your magic powers. But I don't believe it. Is it true you can turn yourself into anything?"

"Of course it's true!" thundered the ogre, opening the door.

"Show me!" challenged Puss.

He was such a boastful ogre. With one roar he became a lion. Puss leapt for his life onto the castle roof.

"Very good!" Puss clapped his paws. "But you can't go from being a mighty lion to a teeny-weeny mouse, can you?"

"But of course," squeaked the ogre, instantly becoming a mouse.

"Got you!" cried Puss, and he pounced and ate him up.

The miller's son could hardly believe it when the King's carriage pulled up in front

of the huge castle and
there was Puss, bowing and
scraping as he welcomed in
the King's party. He set them
before a table groaning beneath a splendid
banquet – which had actually been the
ogre's supper.

"Sir, I'd like you to marry my daughter,"
drooled the King, wiping the wine from his
mouth.

"Sire, I'd be delighted," said the miller's
son, who had fallen as much in love with
the Princess as she had with him.

So they married. And as for Puss, he got a new pair of boots and never chased mice again – except for fun.

The Simple Saame Man
A STORY FROM FINLAND

A Saame man lived in the forest with his
clever wife and his pretty daughter, Nastai.
Being a simple fellow, the man was content
to let his wife be in charge of everything.
She knew where to hunt and fish, set the
traps and knot the nets; it was she who
herded the reindeer, cured the furs and made
the clothes and cooked the meals and kept
the fire going.

One sad day, Nastai's mother died. Now it was Nastai who had to do everything. So she did – and did it well.

After some time, a beggar woman and her daughter arrived. They had heard about the man who, despite being simple, did very well for himself. They plotted to get all he had for themselves.

Later, Nastai came in from the forest to find the beggar woman and her daughter sitting on either side of the hearth as though they owned the place.

"Who are you?" gasped Nastai.

"I am now the mistress of the house, and you'll do as I say."

"Father?" Nastai implored.

But her simple father just nodded helplessly.

"You see? He agrees. Now get to the stove and cook us our dinner," shrieked the beastly woman.

Nastai became their slave. She did everything for them and got nothing in return.

But the beggar woman hated Saame land. She hated the wind wailing in the forest; she hated the wolves howling at night; she hated the loneliness. But most of all, she hated Nastai, who was as good and beautiful as the beggar woman's daughter was ugly and ill-tempered.

One day the beggar woman announced,

"We're leaving!" She ordered the simple man to herd together the reindeer, prepare the sleigh and stack it with every single thing in the hut. Then she and her daughter got in the back.

"What about me?" cried Nastai.

"Who wants you?" sneered the evil woman, and she ordered the simple man to whip up the reindeer and get going.

The hut was empty. Nastai wept. "They have taken the nets, traps, reindeer – and father too. How will I live? They have taken everything."

"Not quite everything," said a soft voice.

"Mother?" exclaimed Nastai. She turned but could see no one.

"Look around," said her mother's voice. "They left one thing behind."

Nastai searched high and low. What could it be? Then the sun glinted on a single thread caught in the floorboards. She pulled at it. The more she tugged, the more it unravelled.

"Knot the thread and make a fishing net," said her mother. "Then cast it into the lake."

Nastai obeyed. To her joy, the net was soon jumping with fish. That night she ate a delicious fish stew.

"Now go into the forest and find a young pine. Plait its roots together and make a rope. Then catch a reindeer calf," said her mother's voice.

Nastai obeyed. She made a rope, caught a young reindeer

and tethered it
outside the hut.
The next morning,
she was astonished to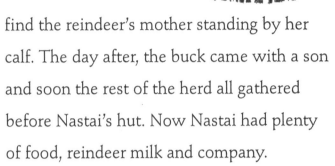
find the reindeer's mother standing by her
calf. The day after, the buck came with a son
and soon the rest of the herd all gathered
before Nastai's hut. Now Nastai had plenty
of food, reindeer milk and company.

Meanwhile, the beggar woman and her
daughter had soon spent the simple man's
wealth. Once more they were dirt poor
and close to starving. They had only one
reindeer left. The woman ordered the simple
man to harness it up. "We shall go back to
your hut. At least we'll have a roof over our
heads. Nastai must be dead."

So back they all went. But what a surprise.

As they came near the hut, they saw a herd of reindeer grazing quietly; a coil of smoke spiralled from the chimney and a delicious smell of cooking came through the open door. They burst inside. Nastai beamed all over at the sight of her father.

"Good!" exclaimed the beggar woman. "We have everything we need."

For the first time in his life, the simple man spoke and took charge. "Oh no, you don't! This is my hut. Get out, beggar woman, and take your horrible daughter with you."

He kicked the two of them out and slammed the door.

Nastai gave her father the best fish stew of his life, and from then on they lived in happiness.

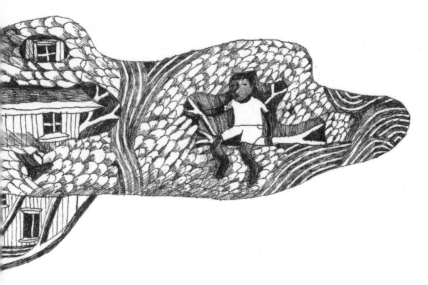

The Witch of the Sands

A STORY FROM BOTSWANA

On the far side of the Singing Sands, where
the sound of one step upon the shining white
grains can be heard a hundred miles away,
lived an evil witch who liked to steal children.

It was because of this witch that a desert
herdsman decided to build a tree house for
his three young motherless sons. He built it

high in the branches of an acacia tree, and the only way up or down was by a rope ladder.

Every day, the herdsman warned his sons, "While I'm away, don't let down the ladder to anyone except me. You will know when I come, for I will whistle three times."

The boys promised. So every day, when their father herded his cattle into the desert to graze, the boys would scamper about among the branches, happy as can be. And every evening, they let down the rope ladder when they heard their father whistle.

But one day the evil witch came and sat in the deep shade of the acacia tree. She knew that, above her head, three pairs of eyes gazed down at her.

"Little boys," she croaked, "let down the ladder so I can come up and see your wonderful tree house." But because they did not hear the whistle, the boys did not let down the ladder.

The wicked witch hid. The next evening when the father came home she heard him whistle three times, and down tumbled the ladder.

"Aha!" the witch gloated. "That's what I'll do!"

The boys told their father about the old woman. "Beware," he said. "It could have been the wicked witch of the Singing Sands."

The next day, when the father had gone into the desert, the witch came back. She whistled three times. Down came the ladder and the witch climbed up.

"Now I've got you!" she screamed, and tucking two boys under one arm and one under the other, she made off.

When the herdsman came home, he saw the dangling ladder.

He knew that something terrible had happened. The tree house was empty and his little boys gone. He thought his heart would break. He ran, howling, into the desert. "Has anyone seen my boys?"

The father ran to the door of a wise man and fell at his feet. "Help me, help me! My three sons have disappeared. I fear they have been stolen by the wicked witch of the Singing Sands. What shall I do?"

"There is only one way to get them back, and that is to kill the witch. The only way to kill her is to break her magic stick in which all her powers lie. There is only one way to cross the Singing Sands without her hearing you, and that is to take my golden drum and beat it with this stick," the wise man said.

The herdsman rubbed ash in his hair to make it grey, and hid the golden drum under a cloak. Disguised as an old man, he set off towards the Singing Sands.

When he got to that shining white place, before he put one foot upon the sands, he began to beat the magic drum.

As soft as a heartbeat, he crossed the Singing Sands.

On the other side he saw the witch's hut. He hobbled up to her door. "Oh! My aching stomach! Would a kind person have a crumb of food for a starving old man?"

"I didn't hear you coming," screamed the witch. "Begone!" But then she caught a glimpse of the golden drum beneath his cloak. She wanted it. "On second thoughts..." She gave a crocodile smile. "I may have a morsel left over. Come on in."

There was a cauldron bubbling, and the witch stirred it with her magic stick. Glowing in a dark corner were three pairs of frightened eyes, and the herdsman knew he had found his boys.

"Mmm! That smells good," he said, putting his nose into the steam.

"You can taste some when I've mixed in this powder," said the witch, thinking she could poison the old man and steal his drum. For a moment, she set down her magic stick to sprinkle in the poison. In that instant, the herdsman snatched up the stick and snapped it across his knee. The witch screamed, but before she could say a word, she crumbled into a pile of dust.

The herdsman joyfully hugged his sons and led them back across the shining white Singing Sands. He didn't bother to beat the golden drum. Everybody heard them coming and rejoiced.

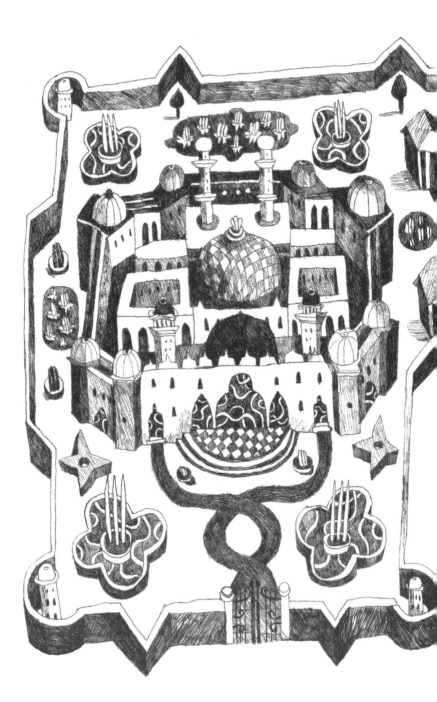

The Paradise City

A STORY FROM MOROCCO

There was once a king who ruled over
a vast and prosperous land. Not only was
he wealthy beyond compare, but he had a
beautiful wife, two noble sons and a glorious
palace, with courtyards and gardens that
were the finest in the Arab world.

But the King was not satisfied. He was
sure he could have something better.

He questioned scholars and wise men; he pored over manuscripts and books; he asked every visitor who passed through his city if they had seen a better kingdom than his.

"No, my Lord," they invariably replied. "We have seen nothing to compare with this."

Then one day, the King came across a huge, dusty book lying hidden in a corner of the library. He opened the book and began to read. He read about a place called Paradise. Nowhere was more beautiful than Paradise; it was more beautiful than anything on Earth, and it was where the good people went after death. The more he read, the more he tried to picture what Paradise was like.

Surely the palaces in Paradise would be built from silver and gold with diamond-studded courtyards; the gardens would be running with cool streams, shaded by rare trees and nodding with sweet-smelling flowers. Surely nowhere on Earth would be happier and more tranquil?

He was determined he would build such a place. He would create Paradise on Earth.

The King summoned his courtiers and noblemen, his architects and craftsmen, and ordered them to build him a city full of shimmering palaces and glorious courtyards. There must be palaces of light and air and water and marble, wood, gold and silver, embedded with the finest metals and jewels. Towers and pinnacles should pierce the clouds; city walls should glitter with precious stones which could be seen from horizon to horizon; there must be gardens so perfumed that songbirds would fly in from every corner of the globe and never wish to leave.

"But Sire," protested the Chief Architect, "you already have the finest city of palaces and gardens in all the world. How can we build anything better?"

The King roared, "Go and do as I have decreed!"

So the builders and craftsmen, architects and labourers searched to the ends of the Earth to find the most precious materials the world could offer. Bit by bit, palaces went up – a hundred of them – one for each

of the King's nobles. They had pillars of
ruby and opal, and floors inlaid with amber
and amethyst. The rooms shimmered with
sapphire, topaz, tourmaline and emerald.

The years went by, and still the building
continued. The gardens were laid out:
fountains sprouting perfume, streams
running with diamonds, and trees, shrubs
and flowers of such rare beauty that the
songbirds sang like angels.

So involved was the King with building
Paradise, he hardly noticed when his wife
died, and his sons went away to seek
their fortunes, and his friends and advisors
gradually withered away.

When at last the city was complete, the King, now old, decreed there should be a magnificent opening ceremony. He would go in procession to see his creation. With his armies, servants and courtiers, he rode to the golden gates of his glorious city.

"Look!" he cried, his voice booming among the lonely towers. "Isn't this the most magnificent palace to be found anywhere on Earth or in Heaven?"

The empty rooms echoed with his pride

and arrogance.

"Have I not built Paradise itself?"

Barely had the words escaped his lips, than the sky darkened. A dreadful sound rumbled below them, and the walls began to shake. The horses neighed and the people trembled.

"Look!" cried a voice shaking with fear. Everyone stared in horror as the ground cracked and opened beneath their feet. The Paradise gardens, the wonderful palaces, the towers of the jewelled city, all the people and animals – everything – began to sink into the earth.

"My dream, my dream!" wept the greedy King, as he too was swallowed up.

Nothing remained. Not one shrub or songbird or bubbling stream; not one minaret or glittering jewel or marble stone. Nothing was left of the Paradise city but the desert sands shifting over the traces, and the wind moaning over the dunes.

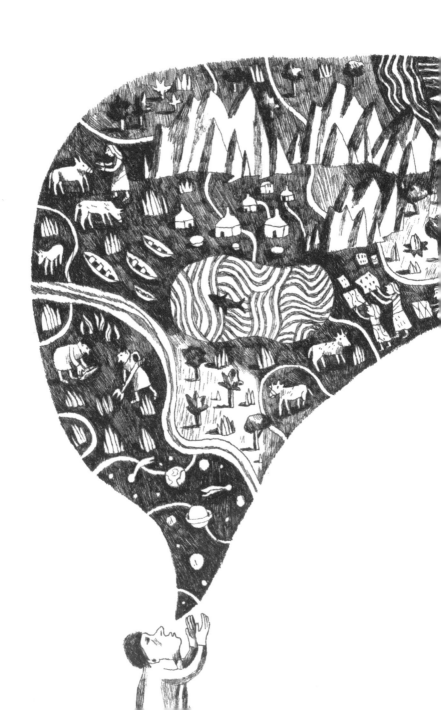

The Birth of Krishna

A STORY FROM INDIA

Kansa was a wicked king who lived long ago.
One day, he was told by a soothsayer that
he would be killed by the eighth child born
to his sister, Devaki. Kansa was outraged
and had Devaki and her husband, Vasudeva,
guarded day and night. He ordered that any

baby born be destroyed, and Devaki's first seven children were killed at birth.

Kansa hoped to keep his evil plan a secret. He threatened to kill his guards if any of them said a word. He didn't want the gods to hear of it. But they did. Lord Vishnu, the Preserver, the god of Goodness and Mercy, who has the power to be born again many times and in many ways, decided he would be born as Devaki's eighth child and went to become Devaki's embryo baby.

When Devaki's eighth child was due to be born, Kansa took no chances. He had Devaki and Vasudeva thrown into the dungeons. An armed guard was placed, day and night, outside the locked door.

It was the middle of the night. A strange calm hung over the world. It was so still that not even a breath of wind stirred the dusty ground. Devaki cried out. The dark, moist body of a boy wriggled into the world and the universe shivered with excitement. In Heaven, drums thudded wildly. Lord Indra scattered a shower of flowers and raindrops out of the sky. Goddesses, angels, nymphs and holy men burst out singing. "Lord Vishnu has been born again as a man, and his name is Krishna!"

Vasudeva held his son fearfully. How could he save their baby?

Suddenly, Krishna opened his eyes. It was like the windows of Heaven opening; it was like a key turning in a lock. Devaki and Vasudeva were amazed as the chains fell from their bodies

 and the prison door flew open. Outside, the guards were slumped in deep slumber.

"Quick! Save our baby!" whispered Devaki. The tears streamed down her face, for she longed to keep him and nurse him and kiss him.

For a moment, the family embraced, then Vasudeva fled with his son into the night. He ran till he came to the banks of the River Yamuna. If only he could get across, they would be safe, for on the other side lived a cowherd and his wife called Nanda and Yasoda. They were good, honest people who would care for Krishna as if he were their own child.

Vasudeva waded into the water. He was halfway across, when a storm blew up. The waters churned angrily.

Soon Vasudeva had to hold his baby high above his head. He thought the end had come and they must both drown, when Krishna stretched out a toe and dipped it into the waves. Miraculously, the swirling waters dropped away, and Vasudeva waded safely out on the other side.

Nanda and Yasoda took the baby. "Don't worry," they murmured. "We will treasure him like a god." Vasudeva thanked them and returned to his wife.

So Krishna was brought up as the son

of a cowherd. He romped and played and was good and bad like any other human child. Sometimes he was very naughty. His name could be heard, ringing out across the meadows. "Krishna is a naughty boy! Krishna is stealing milk from the milkmaids and butter from their churns! Krishna is hanging on to cows' tails so they can drag him through the grass!"

"Is it true, Krishna?" his mother would ask, and he would flash his black eyes and peal with laughter so that his pearly teeth shone like stars. No one could be angry with him for long.

Yasoda hoped and feared for him like any mother. She warned him of dangers, like the demon ogress who ate children and the *naga* that lived on the river bank.

One day, the village children rushed up to Yasoda and told her that Krishna had been eating chalk.

"Is it true? Have you been eating chalk?" she asked.

"No, it's not true," declared Krishna. "The children just want to get me into trouble."

"Open your mouth. Let me see!" cried Yasoda.

Krishna opened his mouth. Yasoda gazed inside. Time and Space stood still. She gazed into the mouth of eternity.

She saw the creation of Heaven and Earth. She saw the planets and the galaxies of the universe. She saw Earth, Water, Fire and Air. She saw volcanoes and earthquakes, mountain ranges thrusting upwards, rushing rivers, jungles, deserts and shining oceans. She saw her own village and the herdsmen tending their flocks. She saw Life and Death.

Yasoda was gazing at creation itself in the mouth of Lord Vishnu. She understood that she didn't need to protect Krishna – he would protect her.

Krishna shut his mouth, and Yasoda immediately forgot everything she had seen. But her heart overflowed with love for him. She took him on her lap and was never afraid again.

Gulnara the Warrior

A STORY FROM MONGOLIA

Gulnara and her sisters lived in a *ger* on
the Mongolian plain with their father and
one chestnut horse. One day, a messenger
ordered the men out to fight in the Khan's
army. Gulnara's father wrung his hands.
"I'm an old man. I'd be no use."

"Too bad!" declared the messenger. "An
order is an order. Obey, or the Khan's men
will slit your throat."

"Don't worry, father!" cried his eldest daughter. "I will go in your place." She took her father's bow and sword, jumped on the chestnut's back and galloped off.

She rode until she came to the Iron Mountain. Blocking her way was an evil black fox with a tail three leagues long. The chestnut reared in terror and raced back home.

"Let me go, father!" said the second daughter. She took up the bow and sword, leapt upon the chestnut and galloped off. She came to the Iron Mountain. Blocking

her way
was a huge
wolf, with
a tail three leagues long. The chestnut horse
reared with fright and galloped home. Father
wailed. "This isn't woman's work. If I don't
go, the Khan's men will slit my throat."

Gulnara stepped forward. "I am the
youngest, but I am taller and stronger than
my sisters. I'm sure I'll get across the Iron
Mountain." With bow and sword, Gulnara
jumped onto the chestnut and galloped off.
The Iron Mountain rose before her.
Blocking the
track was a
huge stag with
six deadly antlers.
The horse pawed the air.

"Stay calm," murmured Gulnara, "so I can fit an arrow to my bow." Her soft words quietened her steed. Gulnara fired. Each arrow hit its mark. The dreadful creature crashed to the ground, dead. Triumphantly, Gulnara entered the pass. The sky darkened. A huge swan swept down. Gulnara fitted an arrow, but the swan called, "Stop! I have come to thank you for killing the stag and releasing me from his power. Take my feather; it will give you my powers." A white feather spiralled to the ground. Gulnara slid it in her shirt, then rode over the Iron Mountain.

The Khan was feasting in his iron tent when Gulnara strode in.

"What lord are you, who does not bow before me?" he bellowed.

"I am no lord, just a maid, and I bow before no man. I have come to fight as you ordered."

"I asked for no woman. In any case, my armies have already left to fight the Khan Kuzlun."

"Then I'd better catch up with them," declared Gulnara. She rode until nightfall, when she found the Khan's army at a thundering river. On the other side was Khan Kuzlun's army. The generals were in despair. "How can we cross this river?"

Gulnara pressed the swan's feather. Immediately, she turned into a swan, flew over the torrent and landed outside Khan Kuzlun's tent.

Khan Kuzlun was talking to his wife. "We can cross the river by the horsehair bridge at the Iron Poplar Tree."

"What if the Great Khan's men find the bridge?"

"Then I will turn our armies into ashes, myself into a camel, you into iron and our daughter into a silver birch."

Gulnara flew back to the other side and became a maid once more. She woke the generals and showed them where to cross the river. All they found at the enemy camp was a pile of ashes, a camel, a lump of iron and a silver birch. "You've made a fool of us!" the generals roared.

Gulnara tied the camel to her horse's tail,

put the lump of iron in her pocket, gathered the ashes into her saddlebag and tucked the silver birch under her arm. Then she rode back and presented them to the Khan. In an instant they were transformed. There stood Khan Kuzlun, his wife and daughter, and nine thousand soldiers. Everyone was amazed.

"Gulnara!" they cried. "What should we do?"

"Peace is better than war," she replied. "Make friends."

So the Khans made friends, and Gulnara galloped home on her chestnut horse.

Rona and the Moon

A STORY FROM NEW ZEALAND

On the northern shore of North Island,
by a stretch of silver beach, lived a Maori
woman called Rona. She lived with her
husband and two sons – and what a happy
life they led!

Every day, Rona's husband and the other
warriors took their canoes out fishing, while
their young sons swam with the dolphins.

Every evening, Rona made sure the cooking stones were just hot enough to make a delicious meal of the fresh fish her husband would bring home.

Everything would have been perfect but for one thing. Rona had such a bad temper. For no reason at all, she could fly off the handle. But her husband and children loved her all the same.

One summer's night, the moon was full and so bright that the fish rose to the surface of the sea, their silver scales flashing.

"This is a perfect night for fishing," said Rona's husband. "I will take the boys out with the warriors in the boat. We'll fish all night and all day tomorrow and be back the same time tomorrow night. We'll be starving, so make sure the cooking stones are just right so that we can cook our catch immediately."

Rona promised, thinking she would enjoy being alone for a while. She slept all night and didn't wake until the sun was high. She meandered about all day, collecting wood for the fire and heating the cooking stones. From time to time, she dashed water on the stones. Nothing made her husband angrier than stones so hot they burnt the fish.

The sun dipped golden into the sea.

The rising moon mixed silver with gold.

Dazzled, Rona fell into a dream.

"Heave-ho! Home we go!"

The voices of father and
sons rang through the night
as their paddles cut into the
water. Rona woke with a start.

How long had she been asleep? Now there
was no golden sunlight – just a dark sea and
the silver moon. She rushed over to her fire.
It was burning brightly, but – oh no! The
cooking stones were blazing hot. She hadn't
cooled them for hours, and both water

gourds were empty.

"Heave-ho!" The
voices were nearer,
hungry and keen

to get home for that delicious fish dinner. Panic-stricken, Rona grabbed the gourds and ran towards the spring.

It was a rocky path and uphill all the way. She scrambled and stumbled, cursing and swearing, but reached the spring and filled her gourds to the brim. Heaving one on each hip, she set off back down the rocky path. At the steepest point, the moon disappeared behind a cloud, plunging Rona into pitch darkness. She tripped and fell. Her gourds smashed. The water sloshed out. Bashed and bruised, Rona scrambled to her feet. Mockingly, out came the moon again.

Rona was furious. "You blithering idiot! You useless piece of rock in the sky! Look what you made me do by hiding your light!" she screamed. "Pokokōhua, cooked head!"

The moon was usually a calm sort of body, drifting above the petty affairs of life, but Rona's insults were too much. It spun down out of the sky and, before she could say "pokokōhua" one more time, swept her upwards.

"Oh, no you don't!" shrieked Rona, grabbing the branches of a ngaio tree and hanging on for dear life.

"Oh, yes I do!" boomed the moon, and with one more mighty tug yanked Rona into the heavens.

When father and sons returned, they found a blazing fire, and stones too hot for cooking. But where was Rona? They searched from sunrise to sunset, shouting her name. Darkness fell. They collapsed exhausted on the ground and stared up at the starry sky.

"The moon!
Look at the moon!"
they cried.

On the glistening
orb was the shape of a
woman clasping two gourds,
one under each arm. Rona must have cursed
once too often. Now she was doomed to
float through the skies for ever and ever.

"Kia mahara ki te hē o Rona," say the
Maoris. "Remember what happened to
Rona."

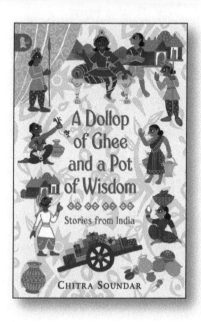

Here is a bunch of dung-dropping, sweet-stealing, luck-jinxing villains!

**A thieving cook,
a greedy sweetshop owner,
a miserly moneylender ...
and more!**

Only Prince Veera knows how to settle the problems in his father's court.

JAMILA GAVIN was born in India and moved to the UK as a teenager. She studied music, then worked for the BBC before becoming a full time writer of stories and plays for children. She is now one of Britain's most acclaimed children's authors, winning the Whitbread Award and being shortlisted for the Carnegie Medal for her novel *Coram Boy*, which was later staged at the National Theatre. Jamila lives in Gloucestershire.

SUZANNE BARRETT grew up in Gloucester and moved to London to study at Central Saint Martins. She likes drawing people, places where people live, and everyday objects and stories. Suzanne has illustrated for magazines, newspapers and books for adults, but this is her first book for children.